The Ballad of M

Written and illustrated by
Pierre Houde

Translated from the French by Alan Brown

La ballade de Monsieur Bedon
Original edition

The Ballad of Mr. Tubs
Translation by Alan Brown

This translation was completed with the assistance of the Canada Council.

Canadian Cataloguing in Publication Data

Houde, Pierre, 1957–
[La ballade de Monsieur Bedon. English]
The ballad of Mr. Tubs

Translation of: La ballade de Monsieur Bedon.
ISBN 0–7710–4225–6 (bound) 0-7710-4226-4 (pkt.)

I. Title. II. Title: La ballade de Monsieur Bedon. English.

PS8565.07635B3413 1988 jC843'.54 C88–094354–8
PZ7.H674Mr 1988

Typeset by VictoR GAD studio
Printed and bound in Canada

McClelland and Stewart
The Canadian Publishers
481 University Avenue
Toronto, Ontario
M5G 2E9

Mr. Tubs is a big, fat man as round as a potato, with a head as bald as an egg. Behind his granny glasses his eyes often light up with pleasure: Mr. Tubs is a great dreamer. Sometimes in the middle of a conversation he will begin to smile for no reason at all and stare at you in a very gentle way. And then he forgets to answer the question you asked. And you say to yourself, "Aha! Tubs is daydreaming again!"

Mr. Tubs is also a great musician. He writes very pretty melodies. He plays the tuba, and he's an excellent music teacher. Many young pupils take lessons from him in his home, and they all pay close attention to what he says.

When Tubs is pleased with his pupils – or with himself – he pats himself on his fat stomach, which is as round as a big note of his music.

Mr. Tubs also likes to eat. He likes it too much, say his young friends. "If he doesn't lose some of his tubbiness, he'll never manage to fly." For our Mr. Tubs has a great dream: he wants to fly around the world. "When you're high in the sky," Tubs explains, "you hear the music the Earth makes all the time. The Earth is a great musician," he often says.

Then one of his pupils will ask him, "What kind of music does the Earth make?"

"Oh," he replies, "it's magnificent music, extraordinary music!" And his face turns red at the thought of it.

"But how does the Earth make music?"

"Well, the Earth is a veritable orchestra: it can produce a whole series of different notes and sounds. Listen to the ocean: when it is calm, its waves sing a soft melody, like an endless cradle song. If it rains in one place, we hear delicate little pizzicato notes, like plucked strings. Where it hails, there is a sound like thousands of tiny bells. If there are many clouds in the air, the Earth will sigh. And if the Earth looks long at its friend the moon, there will be a deep silence."

"And what if there's a storm?"

"Oh, then we hear the loudest music, nothing but rumbles and crashes!"

"And it's only when we're up in the sky that we can hear the whole symphony?"

"Yes, only if we're very high in the heavens do we catch the notes that come from all parts of the world."

And Mr. Tubs rubs his tubby tummy for a moment, lost in his daydream. . . .

"Mr. Tubs, have you ever heard the Earth music?"

"Er . . . no, I heard just a little bar or two. But it was beautiful! And, you know, I've tried everything to get up in the sky."

When Mr. Tubs is not there, his pupils discuss the various unlucky attempts their music teacher has made to attend the concert of the Earth.

"I remember seeing him with great, big butterfly wings, taking off in the air. . . . "

"Well, what happened?"

"Our Mr. Tubs is too heavy. He could barely get off the ground."

"And I remember how he made a giant kite. And I saw him fly with it once when the wind was strong. But he soon came down again. The wind was so powerful it tore the canvas. The kite looked like a big, droopy flower."

"Well, I once helped him to blow up a whole bunch of balloons. We tied them all together and they looked like a cluster of grapes. Mr. Tubs rose up very, very high. . . . "

"And did he hear the Earth music?"

"Just a few notes. You see, up there the sun began to burst his balloons one by one, like popcorn."

"Poor Mr. Tubs!"

In the evenings, when the bats dance across the face of the moon, Mr. Tubs watches the ballet of little notes that fly up from his tuba.

I'll never get to hear the music of the Earth, he thinks sadly.

But suddenly his face lights up: he has just had an idea.

The soft air of night is like a warm blanket on the countryside. A few stars are winking and blinking.

The frogs are wondering, “What kind of light is that, burning so late? And what is that strange music?” It’s Mr. Tubs working all night on his idea.

Next day a whole parade of young musicians marched up the long road leading to Mr. Tubs's house. Each child had brought his own musical instrument: flute or oboe, trombone or trumpet, horn or bassoon, saxophone or clarinet. All the most beautiful wind instruments.

Mr. Tubs met his guests in the park that surrounded his house. Beside him stood a mysterious object that was hidden by a bedsheet. He smiled when he saw how curious the children were about it. Then he gave each child a copy of his latest composition called "Ballad for Wind Instruments." And, with a flamboyant gesture, he unveiled the thing that was hidden under the sheet. What was it? A tuba! A giant tuba, shining in the sunlight. The children were fascinated.

"My friends," said Mr. Tubs with a little teardrop in his voice, "I am about to leave on a long voyage. And we're going to say farewell by playing this ballad together."

When all the musicians were ready and everyone was quiet, Mr. Tubs waved his conductor's baton. At once a wave of beautiful and powerful music flooded the park. The tall grass shivered with pleasure, and the butterflies chased the bubbly, round notes that rose into the air. The giant tuba sent out giant notes, as tubby and round as Mr. Tubs's paunch.

Suddenly Mr. Tubs noticed a few notes flying by that were even bigger than the rest. He grasped two of them, slung one leg over a third note, and let them carry him up into the air. Behind his granny glasses his eyes lit up with pleasure.

Below him, in the park, the children jumped for joy and watched, amazed, as the last notes disappeared into the clouds. They could all imagine how happy Mr. Tubs must be. Far up in the sky he would at last be able to hear the concert of the Earth.

About Pierre Houde

Pierre Houde began drawing when he was seven years old and read his first *Adventures of Tintin* comic book. For him there were always two goals: to tell a story and to put that story into pictures. In 1980 he participated as a colour illustrator in creating the sets in *Heavy Metal*, an animated feature film made in Montreal. Thereafter, he began a close collaboration with the illustrator Raymond Lebrun, and they have covered many different aspects of illustration: animated films, advertising and television.

The Ballad of Mr. Tubs is Pierre Houde's first book, written and illustrated by him. Upon publication in French in 1985, it was highly praised and selected by the Quebec Books for Youth Committee. It has since been released in video, in French and English.